Favorite Fairy Tales
HANSEL AND GRETEL

Retold by Rochelle Larkin   **Illustrated by Alan Leiner**

CREATIVE CHILD PRESS
is a registered trademark of Playmore Inc.,
Publishers and Waldman Publishing Corp., New York, N.Y.

Once upon a time a brother and sister named Hansel and Gretel lived in a little house in a forest. Every day the little boy and girl had to go further and further into the forest to find food for the family.

Their father worried about them because many strange tales were told about mysterious things happening deep in the forest.

"Be sure you mark the way you go very carefully as soon as you leave the house," father said every morning when he went to work, "and be sure to start back for home long before it begins getting dark."

Hansel had a pocketful of bread crumbs that he dropped as they walked in order to mark their way home. They searched for mushrooms, for nuts and berries, and for wild vegetables to make good hearty meals. But it was autumn and food was getting scarcer and they had to go very far to find enough for dinner.

"Remember what father said about getting home before dark," Gretel said.

"I know," said Hansel, "but we haven't got nearly enough yet. Father must have a good dinner before he can go to work again."

"We must start back now, Hansel," said Gretel at last. She was trying not to eat any more of the berries they had picked.

"You're right," said Hansel, looking up at the sky. But when they started back, the bread crumbs he had set out so carefully were all gone! Birds had swooped down and eaten all the crumbs.

They hurried on. But it was growing darker and all the trees seemed the same to Hansel. He couldn't tell which ones they had passed before. "Look over there!" said Gretel suddenly. "I don't remember seeing that clearing, do you?"

Hansel peered into the darkness. Everywhere they had been that day had been thick with trees. He was sure they hadn't passed any cleared spaces. He took Gretel's hand and together they approached the clearing.

There, up a little path through the clearing, was a small house. Its bricks were all made of chocolate and its roof was tiled with row upon row of red jellybeans. Fluffy white marshmallows outlined the windows and peppermint candy canes lined the path to the almond bark door.

Gretel rubbed her eyes. She couldn't believe it. Hansel rubbed his stomach. He couldn't believe it either. "I'm so hungry!" he said. He broke off a little piece of chocolate from a corner of the house. "Here, Gretel, have some."

"But Hansel, we don't know whose house this is!" said Gretel. But she was too hungry to resist. She took the tiniest piece and swallowed it quickly. "Let's go," she said. "I'm afraid."

"As well you should be, you bad little girl!" a strange voice cackled from within the house. Hansel grabbed Gretel and they started to run.

But it was too late. In a twinkling a wicked looking witch stood in the path, blocking their way.

"If you like my house enough to eat it," the witch said, "wouldn't you like to step inside?"

"No, thank you, ma'am," Gretel replied. "We didn't mean to bother you or your house. We —"

"Inside!" roared the witch. She pushed the children in!

It was dark inside, and nothing like the candy out front. The only light came from a great roaring fire in the back. Over the fire hung a huge kettle. The witch grabbed each of the children by a shoulder and pushed them into wire cages. "This is your new home," she cackled, "and here you'll stay till you're plump enough to eat!"

Every night the witch gave Hansel and Gretel huge platters of food to fatten them up.

But every week when the witch would check to see if they had grown plump enough to eat, Hansel and Gretel would hold out sticks instead of their arms.

"We are still too thin to eat," they cried.

Finally the witch grew tired of waiting. She set a great fire roaring in the oven and decided it was time to eat her little prisoners.

But when the witch opened the cages, Hansel and Gretel, who had grown very strong from all that good food, pushed the witch herself right into the oven.

They raced home and told their father all about their amazing adventure. And after that, Hansel and Gretel returned many times to snack on the witch's candy house.